H589s

Sky All Around

ANNA GROSSNICKLE HINES

CLARION BOOKS • NEW YORK

For Lassen and Gary, who started it,
and for Jim and Carol, who helped complete it.

Clarion Books
a Houghton Mifflin Company imprint
52 Vanderbilt Avenue, New York, N Y 10017

Text and Illustrations copyright © 1989 by Anna Grossnickle Hines

Library of Congress Cataloging-in-Publication Data

Hines, Anna Grossnickle.
Sky all around / Anna Grossnickle Hines.
p.   cm.
Summary: A father and daughter share a special time when they go
out on a clear night to watch the stars.
ISBN 0-89919-801-5: $13.95
[1. Fathers and daughters—Fiction.   2. Stars—Fiction.]
I. Title.
PZ7.H572Sk   1989   88-16966
[E]—dc19
AC

It was Mommy's turn to give the baby his bath and Daddy's time for me. He was pushing me in the swing, up so high my toes could almost touch the trees.

Then I saw it.

"Look, Daddy. Look! The moon is shining and it's not even dark yet! It's a tiny little sliver moon."

"Umhmm," Daddy said, "a crescent moon. Tonight will be good for watching the stars."

"Can we?" I said. "Please?"

So Daddy got our sweaters and I got the flashlight. We walked up the road, just Daddy and me. And the moon came, too.

We climbed up the hill to our special place and watched

the sky all around as the big orange sun went down.

The birds sang a good-bye song to the day

and the sky turned rosy and violet.

The crickets and the frogs sang a hello song to the night and in the sky the first star shone. Daddy said it was really a planet and its name was Jupiter.

It looked like a star to me. I wished a wish, and Daddy wished one. I think the moon did, too.

We saw another star and another and another, and the moon shone brighter in the deep blue sky. We lay on the grass and listened to the night songs of the frogs and crickets, and watched.

Ten stars, a hundred stars, a thousand stars, a million stars in the nighttime sky.

"What do you see?" Daddy asked.

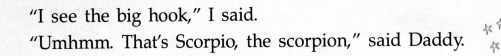

"I see the big hook," I said.

"Umhmm. That's Scorpio, the scorpion," said Daddy.

"And I see the Big Dipper and the North Star. See it, Daddy? Is that it right up there?"

"That's it."

"What else, Daddy?"

"That half-circle of stars over there is the Northern Crown," Daddy said.

"It looks like a princess's crown," I said. "I think I'll wear it."

"All right." Daddy laughed. "You can be my Star Princess."

"It's still in the sky even while I'm wearing it. That's because it's a magic crown. Oooh! A shooting star! Did you see that, Daddy?"

"No, I missed it," said Daddy. "Maybe I'll see the next one. Do you see that teapot over there? It has a triangle for the spout and a triangle for the top."

"I see it! I see the teapot! Would you like some tea, sir? Do princesses serve tea?"

"This princess can do whatever she wants to do,"
Daddy said. "She's a very special princess, wearing a
magic crown."

"Okay, Daddy sir. Here's your tea. Sip it carefully.
It's quite hot, you know."

"Good too," said Daddy, "but I think it's time to go."

"You haven't seen your shooting star yet," I said. "We can't go until you do. It could be very bad luck if you don't see one."

"Who told you that?"

"Nobody. I'm the Star Princess so I just know."

Daddy laughed.

"All right. We'll stay a little bit longer, but I might have to risk my luck until next time."

"Let's find our own pictures, Daddy, and name them whatever we want. I see something that flies and sits on flowers. It looks kind of like two triangles hooked together. Can you guess what it is?"

"A butterfly," Daddy guessed.

"Right!" I said. "Its name is Beautiful-Butterfly-in-the-Night. Okay, now it's your turn."

"I see something that flies too, but it isn't alive and it doesn't have wings."

"Then how can it fly?"

"On the end of a string."

"Is it shaped like a diamond?"

"Umhmm."

"I see it! It's a kite, isn't it, Daddy?"

"You guessed it. Its name is Star Flyer."

"That's a good name," I said. "I see a house lying down."

"I see it too," said Daddy. "What shall we name it?"

"Sleeping House," I said, "and it's our house and we're all inside. You and me and Mommy and baby brother." I yawned.

"You're a sleepy Star Princess," Daddy said. "I really think it's time to go now."

"But you didn't see…Oooooh!"

"Wow!" Daddy said. "That was a great shooting star!"
"You're going to have super good luck, Daddy."
"I already have it," he said.

He carried me piggy-back down the hill and up the road.

I held the flashlight so we could see, and the little crescent moon came, too.

"We saw Jupiter in the sky," I told Mommy, "and
two shooting stars and a teapot and our house lying
down. And the moon came with us all the way."

"Maybe you can show me sometime," Mommy said.
"I will, and brother when he's bigger, and I'll be the
Star Princess again and hold the flashlight on the way
home."